LOSING THINGS
AT MR. MUDD'S

CAROLYN COMAN
PICTURES BY LANCE HIDY

FARRAR, STRAUS & GIROUX
NEW YORK

CURR
P2
C729
O
1992

FOR ANNA & HER
AUNT ANNIE GRACE,
AND FOR LOUIS
& MONTY

When Lucy Farr was six years old, she visited a distant relative whose name was Mudd, Bernard Mudd.

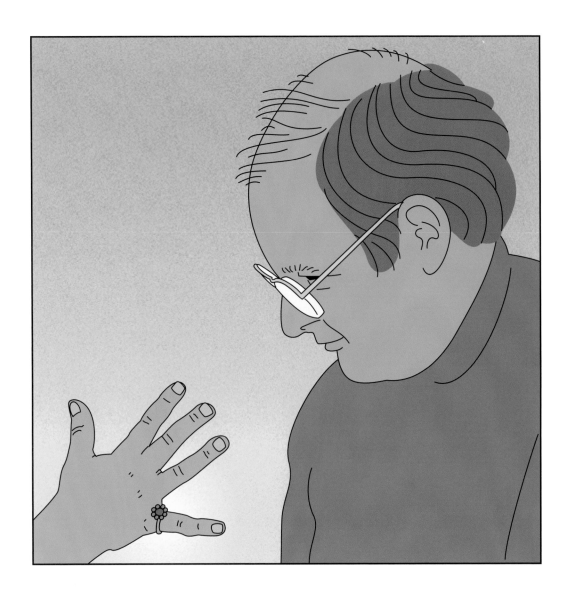

The day that Lucy arrived, Mr. Mudd presented her with a tiny ruby ring. She slipped it on her littlest finger right away.

"Oh, no no no no no," Mr. Mudd chuckled. "No no no no. Have you lost your senses?" he asked her. "Child," he said, reaching out to take the ring off her finger, "one doesn't actually wear this ring. Do you have any idea what a ring like this is worth?"

Lucy did not have any idea.

"It's extremely rare, terribly precious," he told her. "Antique, you know. We'll put it here, for safekeeping." He tucked the ring into a box lined with red velvet and snapped the box shut. Mr. Mudd had a horror of losing things.

Lucy thanked Mr. Mudd, even though she would much rather have worn her ring than trap it inside a box.

Then Mr. Mudd gave Lucy a tour of his house. As he pointed out all the wonderful things he had, he reminded Lucy that she must not touch, or hold, or play with any of them. There were chairs that she was not allowed to sit on and music boxes that she was not allowed to wind up. Even the library was of no use to Lucy. Each time Lucy reached out to pull a book from the shelf, Mr. Mudd would say, "Oh, no no no no, child. Oh, heavens no," and explain that the book she was about to touch was 159 years old and far too delicate for "little hands."

Lucy wondered what good a book was if it couldn't be looked at, and what good a toy was if it couldn't be played with, and what good a ring was if it couldn't be worn, but she didn't say a word.

Mr. Mudd suggested that Lucy run along and play outside. She shot out the door and took a great big breath of fresh air, and then wandered over to the goldfish pond.

Lucy loved the way the fish and pebbles looked in the sunlight. They shone like jewels. She thought of the ruby ring trapped inside the red velvet box, and how it would sparkle in the sun!

Lucy slipped inside the great house. Mr. Mudd was in the dining room, dusting his fancy plates with a special duster made from ostrich feathers. He did not see Lucy sneak in, and he did not see her sneak out, wearing her ring.

She played in the garden for the rest of the morning, and a very sad
thing happened: Lucy lost her ring. She combed every inch of the
garden looking for it, until, at last, she just gave up.

At lunch, Lucy broke the bad news to Mr. Mudd.

"You lost it?" he thundered at her from the head of the table. "You lost it?" he roared again. "Do you know what that ring was worth?" Lucy still had no idea, but it seemed the ring was worth even more to Mr. Mudd now that it was lost.

"I'm sorry," she mumbled.

"Speak up," he shouted.

"I'm sorry," she hollered back at him, feeling less and less sorry every second.

But Mr. Mudd was not listening. He had lost his patience. "Go to your room," he commanded.

Lucy climbed the stairs to her bedroom, closed the door, and flopped down on her bed. She was miserable. Not only had she lost her ring and her temper, but it just so happened that she was close to losing a tooth. She felt as if she was losing everything. "Oh brother," she said, and then let out a big, deep sigh.

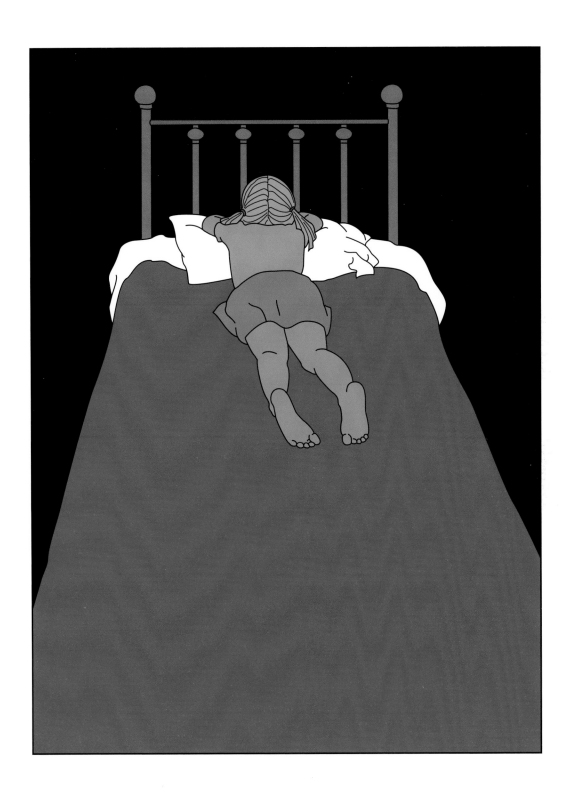

As Lucy sat upstairs trying not to jiggle her tooth any looser, Mr. Mudd searched for the ring. Nothing is lost until you stop looking, he reminded himself. And he was right: later that afternoon, he found the ring on the porch, lying on the straw mat from India that he had put there for people to wipe their dirty feet on. He was very glad to see it, and tucked the ring into his sweater pocket for safekeeping.

This is not the end of the story of losing things at Mr. Mudd's, though, because later that same day, Lucy lost her loose tooth.

At dinnertime, just as Mr. Mudd was lecturing her about the value of things, Lucy sneezed and her tooth came flying out of her mouth and into her hand. Lucy was horrified, and quickly tightened her fist around her tooth.

"Gesundheit," Mr. Mudd called down to Lucy from his end of the table.

Lucy was scared to answer. She didn't want Mr. Mudd to see that she had lost yet another thing.

"Lucy?" Mr. Mudd said. "When one is told gesundheit, one should respond with a thank you."

Lucy mumbled "Thank you" without moving her lips or opening her mouth very much. She looked like she was practicing to be a ventriloquist.

"Speak up, child," he corrected her. "Speak up."

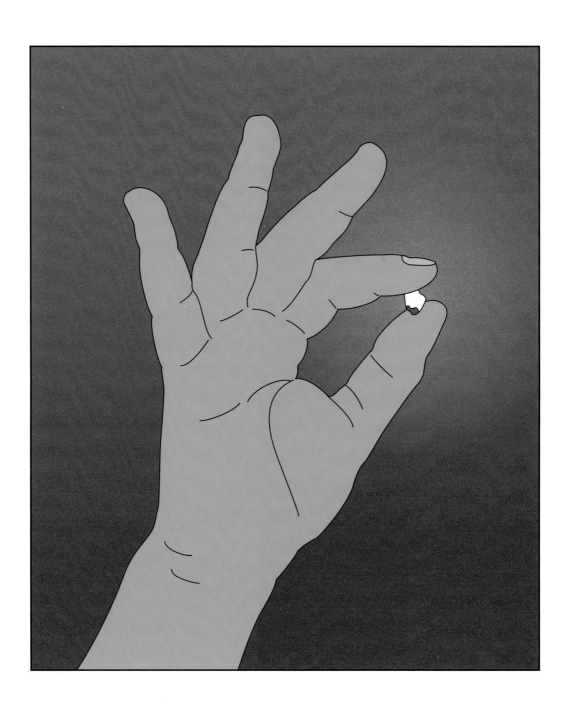

Enough was enough. Lucy Farr had had it. "All right," she said, loud and clear. "I lost my tooth. See?

"And I didn't mean to, but I couldn't help it, and it's my thing, and I wish I never came here to visit you and all your dumb stuff that you don't even use anyway." And then Lucy bared her remaining teeth at Mr. Mudd in the meanest, scariest face that she could make.

The two of them just looked at one another for what seemed like a long time. Then Mr. Mudd closed his mouth, straightened himself up in his chair, and cleared his throat. "Well," he said finally. "Well." Neither of them felt like eating any more of their dinner; they had lost their appetites. Not much later Lucy asked if she could please be excused and go to her room.

"Yes, certainly," Mr. Mudd said. As Lucy was leaving the dining room, Mr. Mudd cleared his throat once again. "Perhaps," he suggested to Lucy, "you might want to put your tooth under your pillow—so that it doesn't get any more lost than it already is." Lucy, who by this time was feeling rotten about her lost ring and her lost tooth and her lost temper, nodded her head. "Good night."

Lucy put her tooth beneath her pillow and went to bed,

and dreamed dreams of losing everything.

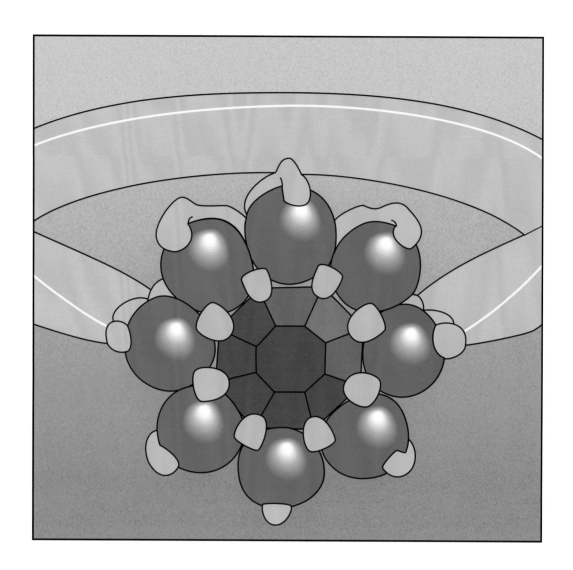

When she woke up, she checked under her pillow right away. But her hand found no tooth. Instead, there was the ruby ring! Lucy could hardly believe her eyes. She was so happy to see it that she went running down the stairs to tell Mr. Mudd.

He sat in his leather armchair in the library, reading the listings of Things for Sale in the newspaper, and looked up only after Lucy had repeatedly tugged on his sleeve.

"What is it, child?" he finally said.

A shy smile spread across her face as she held up the ring to Mr. Mudd.

"Most extraordinary," he said, "most extraordinary." Then he told her that she might as well go ahead and wear the ring after all.

"Do you know what this ring is worth?" Lucy said, sounding just like Mr. Mudd when he asked her that same question.

"Child," he answered her, "I know exactly what your ring is worth."

As Lucy's smile broadened, a window appeared in her mouth where her tooth had been. She told Mr. Mudd she was sorry for the way she had talked to him the night before. Lucy always found it easier to apologize when she wasn't mad.

Mr. Mudd made a funny rumbling noise that sounded like a mix between clearing his throat and talking.

"Pardon me?" Lucy said.

He only made the same sound again.

"Speak up," Lucy said.

"Oh, all right," Mr. Mudd said. "If you must know, I'm sorry, too."

Later on, Lucy and Mr. Mudd wound up every one of his music boxes
and listened to their songs. Mr. Mudd grumbled that he
was probably losing his mind to let a child
handle such valuable items, but he
had to admit that the
music was
sweet.

THIS BOOK WAS DESIGNED AND PRODUCED
entirely on a Macintosh computer by Lance Hidy, Newburyport,
Massachusetts. Design and production help was provided by
Virginia Evans and Rob Day.

The text typeface is ITC Stone Informal, designed by Sumner
Stone of the Stone Typefoundry. The titles are Trajan capitals,
designed by Carol Twombly at Adobe Systems.

Film separations were made by Sanjay Sakhuja and Robert
Matthews at Digital Pre-press International, using a Scitex Dolev PS.
The printing was done by the Stinehour Press, and the binding by
Horowitz/Rae Book Manufacturers.

The pictures were created with Adobe Illustrator and Adobe
Photoshop. The computer was a Macintosh II with a Radius Rocket
accelerator. The Radius display hardware included a 19" monitor, a
24-bit video card, and a PrecisionColor Calibrator. Scanning of 35
mm slides was done on an Array SpeedScanner and a Nikon LS-
3500; drawings were digitized on a Microtek 300Z flatbed color
scanner. Color proofing was done on a Kodak XL-7700 printer.

Thanks to Luanne Cohen and Gail Blumberg of Adobe Systems
for their early guidance; and thanks also for the support
given by Ron Roszkiewicz through the Scitex
America Corporation, and by Mitch Allen
through Eastman Kodak
Electronic Printing
Systems.